Copyright © 2004 by NordSüd Verlag AG, Gossau Zürich, Switzerland
First published in Switzerland under the title *Der Dachs hat heute schlechte Laune!*
English translation copyright © 2004 by North-South Books Inc., New York

First published in the United States, Great Britain, Canada, Australia, and New Zealand in
2004 by North-South Books, an imprint of NordSüd Verlag AG, Gossau Zürich, Switzerland.
First paperback edition published in 2006 by North-South Books.

Library of Congress Cataloging-in-Publication Data is available.
A CIP catalogue record for this book is available from The British Library.

ISBN-13: 978-0-7358-1888-0 / ISBN-10: 0-7358-1888-6 (trade edition) 10 9 8 7 6 5 4 3 2
ISBN-13: 978-0-7358-1889-7 / ISBN-10: 0-7358-1889-4 (library edition) 10 9 8 7 6 5 4 3 2 1
ISBN-13: 978-0-7358-2035-7 / ISBN-10: 0-7358-2035-X (paperback edition) 10 9 8 7 6 5 4 3 2 1
Printed in Denmark

THE BAD MOOD!

By Moritz Petz

Illustrated by Amélie Jackowski

Translated by J. Alison James

North-South Books

New York / London

"Humph!" Badger said to himself when he woke up.
"I'm in a bad mood today! This might be dangerous.
 Maybe I'd better stay at home."

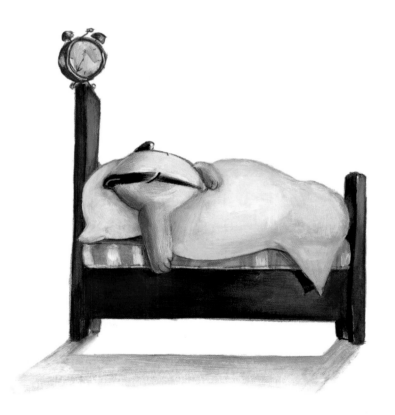

At breakfast, Badger reconsidered. What was the point
of being in a bad mood if nobody noticed? Everybody ought
to know how miserable I feel, he thought. So Badger headed
out, slamming the door behind him.

Badger was going along his usual route when he met Raccoon.

"Good morning, Badger," Raccoon said cheerfully.

"Good morning? What's so good about it?" Badger replied, and stomped off.

Raccoon was so shocked, he didn't say good-bye.

Deer was doing his washing. "Hello there, Badger. Sleep well?"
"None of your business," Badger said.
"Well, excuse me for asking!" said Deer.
Good, thought Badger. Now Deer and Raccoon know I'm in a bad mood.

Badger kept going. On his way he met Mouse and Fox and Hare and Squirrel. He was as rude to them as he could be.

When he was finished with his morning walk, Badger
came back home and started to work in his garden.
 As he was digging and weeding, the strangest thing
happened. His bad mood just slipped right off him, as if it
had been a shirt that was too hot to wear. Badger became
so happy that he started to whistle a sweet song.

Badger didn't stop working until late that afternoon.
He was deeply satisfied with himself. He went out to the
clearing to play with the other animals. But the woods
were still and silent. Not an animal appeared.

Strange, thought Badger. Where are they all?

He went to Raccoon's house to ask.

Raccoon was not in a good mood. "Leave me alone!" he grumbled.

Badger was shocked. No one had ever been so rude to him before.

It wasn't any better with the other animals.
Fox told him to get lost.
Squirrel hurled a nut at his head.
Mouse and Hare shouted and hissed at Badger,
which made him quite dizzy.

Badger was miserable. When Blackbird came to visit, he told her about how mean all the animals had been to him.

"There must be a reason," said Blackbird.

Badger thought about it. "Well," he said finally. "I *was* in a bad mood this morning and I guess I took it out on my friends. I was very rude to them." Badger felt just awful. "Oh, dear! What can I do?"

Blackbird and Badger thought about the problem together. Suddenly Badger jumped up. "I have an idea!" he said. "Will you help me?"

"Indeed I will," said Blackbird.

"Party tonight!" cawed Blackbird as she fluttered through the forest. "Everyone who is in a bad mood is invited! Come to the clearing at moonrise for a bad mood party!"

And since Badger had passed his bad mood on to the other animals they all showed up at the party. When they saw Badger standing in the clearing they glared angrily at him.

Badger took a deep breath. "I want to apologize," he said. "This morning, I was in an awful mood, and I took it out on all of you. You are my friends, and it was a terrible thing for me to do. I am so sorry. Will you please forgive me?"

At last the animals smiled.

Together they sang songs and danced until dawn.